NO CHANCE

Nowhere is home

DEANDRE DORSEY

ISBN
978-1-961601-12-3 (Paperback)
978-1-961601-13-0 (eBook)
978-1-961601-11-6 (Hardcover)

Table of Contents

"This world treats us like prisoners, they give us one of everything and make it their second chance. In this world that I'm making for us there is no such thing as chances".

—Max Colar Sr.

Jr. Ruff School Day

The rain was fulfilling day with unhappiness and trouble the Max Jr. was staring at the window in his class not focusing on school because of his parents' divorce. A classmate name Darcy Allen ask Max "What's wrong"? Nothing. He said. It got to be something you been looking out that window since class started said Darcy. Then a husky young man name k David came along to assaults him "He's a virgin that's all they can do is see and don't touch". The teacher name Ms. Floyd came in to stop the teasing "David that's enough stop it. Darcy looks back at David to flip her middle finger at David he blows a kiss at her to say too bad you can't that to him.

Max decided to fight back even if he has to be suspended from school "Hey David you what they say about guy who talks about sex a lot"? What said k David. They always be virgins everybody in class started to laughs including the lovely Darcy Allen. Ms. Floyd ask both boys to leave the classroom to go up the principal office. As both boys leave the classroom k David ran down Max Jr. turns him over and drive his fist into his face four times. Then Max Jr. turns the table by head butting him on his nose turns him over and start punching him in his nose six times until the school officer ran through the crowd and break up the fight. K David got his ass whoop by the quietly, seen innocently pure Max Colar Jr.

The boys were taking to principal wright office of what was going on that started the fight. "Now what is going on here" said principal wright. He was taking about me so I insult him back said Max Jr. What did he say that made you snap? He calling me a virgin disrespecting my manhood. K David started giggling about his comment. "SHUT UP NOW, DAVID" said principal wright. Now what I'm going have to do is suspend you two for fighting. Thank you so much I really need a vacation said K David with a smart ass attitude. Oh really then you are going to love with its officer dawn put you to work and it starts now you may be excused. "What about olive oil here" said K David Max Jr. turn around with his fist balled up wanting to punch him again. "THAT'S ENOUGH, YOU GOT ONE MORE TIME THEN I'M EXPELLING YOU FROM THIS SCHOOL, try me if think I'm bluffing said the principal with his voice raised high.

K David walk out the door with punishment with the school officer then he turns his attention to Max Jr. asking what is really going on in his personal life. Max what is the problem you've been carrying aburdon your shoulder for weeks? I got personal issues ok, and I don't want talk about it. You know I got to call your parents on what happened here, is it that serious where you taking your rage against everyone? No, right now my parents problems is much bigger then mines said Max Jr. how? I don't want to get into that it hurts when I talk about this. The principal is still trying to figure out Max problems as Max continues setting up brick walls for him not to get inside his world. Do I need to call a doctor a psychiatrist maybe, I know people in that field Max?

Max is getting really inpatient about the questioning from the principal so he got up from his chair pick his book bag. To the principal he said "look thanks but no thanks if I need your help I'll ask for it, just let me go home ok". The principal grants Max Jr. his wish by dismiss him from school Max walk out the school begins walking home with shame and sorrow company him as he faces another battle outside of school. He finally reach home opens the front door walk up stairs to his bedroom closes his door ramble threw his dresser pulls out his joint that he rolled up and begins his smoke. Escape from all the pain from reality that gave him just so he can be in ecstasy for an hour.

After his j smoke was over he went down stairs to the kitchen to grab a granny smith apple and a peter pan peanut butter from the refrigerator. He walk towards the couch sat down cutting the apple in four slices and dip it inside the peanut butter indult it and he begin to stare at a broken frame picture of his mom and dad kissing on the ground glass is still on the ground from the argument that took place last night. Max Jr. finish his snack and begins to take a nap on the couch from having such a very rough day at school. Two hours later Max woke up from his nap and sees his dad looking at him with another bad news.

"Dad what's wrong you now"?

I lost my job at the firm? Max Sr. said with guilt

"What you just got this job like three months ago"?

I know son, I know, I barely got enough money for this divorce? Said Max Sr.

Why you and mom are getting divorce you two promise me that wouldn't happen?

I know that, but your mother said I never was making enough money to keep her happy?

So that's what it boil down to, is money?

Son its' not about the money it's just-

Just what dad?

Max Sr. was running out of answers to his so on why is everything is going bad for him when they just got back on their feet.

So what are going to tell mom when she get here?

I don't know?

Leslie colar walks in the front door rushes upstairs to get the rest of her things while her new husband is waiting in his car.

"Leslie what there something I got to tell you"? Said Max Sr.

"I don't want to talk to you ok I'm just getting the rest of my things ok, I'll see you in court?

"Leslie I just got to tell you that I lost my job today"?

"Well that's on you just get the state to represent you I have to go"?

Max Jr. walk half way up the stairs he hears both of his parents get into an altercation that he heard from last night. Then out of nowhere

Leslie new man rushes into the front door pushes Max Jr. out the way walk up the bedroom door then he kick it open.

"WHAT THE HELL YOU THINK YOU DOING HERE"? Max Sr. yell at him.

"I told him to come in if I take too long "?

Babe what the hell is going on here? Said Sam

I'm trying to get my things but my new ex-husband is making up excuses for me to stay.

Look pal- said Sam

I'm not you're fucking pal! Said Max Sr.

Max Sr. throws the first punch at Sam' hitting him in his lip then Sam threw a punch at him in his stomach. Max Jr. runs to the kitchen and grab the meat cleaver ran upstairs to his parents' bedroom and grabs Sam blonde hair and put the blade across his throat. His mother beg him to put the knife down so he won't kill him. Then his father stands there looking his son in his eyes like he is controlling him Max Jr. puts down the knife and let go Sam. Both father and son watch Leslie runs to her new husband aid her and Sam grab each other and walk out the house. Max Sr. put his right arm over his son shoulder as he cries to see his parents' marriage crumble before his eyes.

Both of the colars went back inside the house filled with disappointment and tragic that Leslie is gone and never coming back to them.

A Friends Death

The next morning after the abruptly night when Max Jr. almost killed his mother new husband he wakes up from his bed to begins his morning with depression. He walks to his bathroom across the hall to sit down on the toilet to take a shit. When he got up from the toilet wipe himself and clean his hands he walk down stairs to see an eviction notice on the front door saying " 1 days for payment or be vacate ". Max Jr. ball up the notice with more frustration added to his anger so he goes to the back yard with his baseball bat and begins bashing the ground with it at least five times letting go his anger the best way he know how.

Until his house phone rings he stops carrying his bat to inside the house picks up the phone rising his voice at the caller.

"WHAT "

"Max calm down its Darcy "?

Oh I'm sorry hi?

"What's going on with you I haven't seen you in school today"?

"I'm suspended why, what are you doing?

I'm on my to work I just left class how many days are you suspended?

I don't know, probably forever?

Yeah right I was going to call you last night but I didn't have time.

I understand what's been going in class before you left?

Everybody is still talking about you how you finally fight back against that "King Dickhead"?

Max Jr. laughs at Darcy humor as they still continues talking on the phone.

So how are you and your boyfriend doing does he know you talks to me more than him? Said Max Jr.

Darcy laughs and said "If he doesn't know he knows now"?

What do you mean?

It means- then the house phone gets cut off Max Jr. was pissed that the service was wasn't paid. He runs back upstairs to charge up his cell phone with 6% percent on there he calls Darcy back but it went to straight to voicemail. He goes inside his parent's room in his dad dresser and grab his last cigarette smoking in the house thinking that Darcy is going to call him back. Three hours later Max Sr. came back from finding a job that fit his requirements but none came available. He sits down on the couch next to his son also having a bad day as well.

Maxy my boy how's it going?

Nothing just enjoying my vacation?

His dad laughs at his son humor "That's good it looks like where both on vacation without pay "?

So when is the court date for you and mom?

It's actually tomorrow you coming?

Do I have a choice? Max looks at his dad in his eyes with his answer.

Huh, yes you do let me get out these clothes so we can get a burger at island restaurant?

Just when he got from his seat he sees a tow truck to see his BMW getting towed Max Sr. and Jr. ran out the front door yelling at the guy asking him "What are you doing "?

You haven't paid your car note pal?

I just made my payment?

Look it shows that you didn't you don't pay you don't drive?

Just give me another day I have to go court tomorrow?

That's not my problem sir.

The tow truck man continues his work towing the car on the truck and drive away without no transportation. Max Sr. stands there angry and frustrated that their day has gone complete sour thinking that their day couldn't get any worse.

Dad, dad lets go back inside?

I need my smokes get in the house now. Said Max Sr.

They gone inside Max Jr. sat back on the couch to turn on the news his dad calls him from his bedroom.

Yeah?

Did you smoke my last cigarette?

I think so?

What do you mean you think so did you or didn't you?

Yes I did.

The angry father went inside his wallet crumble up seven one dollar bills at threw them at him. Doing some bullying because his last cigarette was gone to cool him down. He force Max Jr. to pick up the money to get him some more cigarettes. Max Jr. picks it up then he froze when he saw the breaking news.

"This just been a breaking news a high school student name Darcy Allen was killed today in jackknife with an eighteen wheeler ran into her car in Lomita Blvd. She was only 17 years old then her best friend name Abrigel Thompson has something to say "I'm just very heartbroken at this moment no comment please" as she's crying & grieving over her friend's death. The cause of death was to believe of text or call no further information has not been reviled at this time I'm Kimberly Luo with your evening news.

Max Jr. got back up from the ground went outside to start crying & grieving like his parents died. His dad went outside to sit by his son to comfort his son on another tragedy on this dark day of his. "It was my fault" Said Max Jr. How it is your fault? Said Max Sr.

She was talking to me and I tried to call her back?

No son it's not your fault you was just the last person that she meant to talk you on this day.

Funerals & Courts What's the Different

Next day on a sunny morning of the homecoming of Darcy Allen at Green Hills Memorial Park. Many of her family, friends & strangers of her all gather around her casket. Father Reynolds was there to speak of her.

"Today god's children's we are here to celebrate & remember the life our beloved girl Darcy Stacy Allen she was truly the young lady that everyone want to have as a family member & friend even though she was taken away from us so soon. She was here to love everyone here at her time she will be gone but not forgotten may she live forever in the house of the lord ashes to ashes dust to dust".

Many had morn over the fact that she is never coming back even Max Jr. was there looking all depressed in his black suit. Her mother had some assisted to get up from her seat by Darcy's ex –boyfriend and her father. The day of sadness quickly turns to anger when Max Jr. want to speaks to Darcy's mother and father about his beloved friend. Max Jr. pulls out a beautiful single Ms. Mars Sunflower from his jacket to give to her mother.

Until her ex-boyfriend came into the picture by asking Max "What do you want, man"?

I need to give Darcy's parents this flower because it's hard for-

Max got cut off by Darcy's rude boyfriend "Just give me the flower so I can give to them"?

That's very rude of you cutting me off but you're not her parents so would you mind?

The Darcy 's ex-boyfriend Claude was going to explode & cause a scene with Max. "Look asshole if I was you need to leave before I ". Max Jr. was pulling his card and call him bluff "I WHAT YOU GOING TO KICK MY ASS BECAUSE YOU & EVERYBODY HERE LOST DARCY" Max Jr. shouted at him. Claude punch the hell out of Max Jr. Darcy 's mom ran to the scene while officers retrain both broken hearted boys. "What are you boys doing?" Claude put the blame on Max Jr. about the fight by saying "Mrs. Allen I'm sorry this jerk was threating me before he shouted to everybody". Max Jr. spoke up to defend himself but Darcy's mom cut him from hearing his excuse. Ma'am Claude jus- , so you came to my daughter funeral to start all this trouble"? Mrs. Allen grieving.

No, no I'm not she was special to me Mrs. Allen look at Max Jr. with pain & sorrow in her eyes and said "Leave us alone" pallbearers, her husband,& Claude help Darcy mom to the black limousine. Max Jr. stand there feeling like an outcast an outsider like he was wasn't invited. When everybody drove off Claude the ex-boyfriend turn his head & give Max Jr. the middle finger because the won their trust. Meanwhile at 1: 21 p.m. at the Stanley Mosk Courthouse another Max colar his father was also going to have a dark clouded day as he face his wife Leslie of 15 years. Leslie sat down with two high power attorney while Max Sr. stands there with a lawyer of his own getting ready to end their marriage.

The officer came in and said "All raise the present of our flag of our country emblem of our constitution remember the principle of which takes stand department threw the court is now in section. The honorable Johnathan Mason judge presaging please be seated & come to order". Judge Mason opens his file on Max Colar Sr. & Leslie Colar. Good after noon everyone I see here that Leslie Tracey Colar wants to file for divorce Max Colar Sr. of 15 years. May I ask why? Leslie lawyer freeman got to say "it's believe that her husband Mr. Colar has failed her to be a responsible husband and a father. Max Colar attorney got to say objection you're honorable. Please be seated consular you may continue, thank you your honor. My client want to gain full custody of their son Max Colar Jr. and not to take anything from Mr. Colar because she claim he has nothing to get from Mr. Colar and I quote.

me ". Judge Mason spoke up "Do you work"? Max said "I just lost my job "doing what said Judge Mason. Max Sr. stops and pulse like he was frozen he walks from his table up to the judge and the officer retrain him & told him "Mr. Colar please return to your seat. While Max Sr. steering at the judge Leslie looks at her newly ex-husband worried could make a move that will send him to jail. Max Sr. walks up to the stand and said to the Judge "Your Honor I'm not going to ask any more of your or anybody question about my lifestyle all I have is my son and to answer your UN ask question I'm a great dad. I love my son more than I used to love that unsatisfied nonsupport cunt over there". Leslie stop her lawyer's conversation & got furious when he call a name that every woman hates to be called. "What did you just call me? You call me a what a cunt". She got up and threw her chair at Max Sr. but he duck so the flying chair hit the judge in the face. A few officers ran in the courtroom to arrest both Max Sr. & Leslie for offensive language, damage court property, & assaulting the judge.

Leslie shout out loud "I HOPE OUR SON SEND YOU TO HELL YOU SON OF A BITCH". Two hours later out of bail at Max Sr. was set free while Leslie was not. Max Sr. was waiting for the bus Leslie's fiancée Sam ran up the door & stop turn around looks at Max Sr. as he got on the bus Max Sr. sat down turn his head and stair back at Sam as if both men had unfinished business with one another. Max Jr. was setting on his front steps of his house he calmly smoke a cigarette without no consequence coming. Max Sr. walks up to his son looks at him and said "How was Darcy's funeral?"

Max shakes his head no because it was hard for him to answer his dad like always demand Max Jr. to speak to him. "Max I'm not going ask again tell me now"? Said Max Sr.

I went to a fucking funeral that I wasn't invited. Said Max Jr. as he storms into house both broken-hearted colars had so much hatred to their world is going to collapse.

"Hey don't walk away from me when I'm talking to you boy".

"Look dad I don't want to talk right now "

"In this house you go by my rules not your own."

"DAD I DON'T WANT TO HERE THIS SHIT RIGHT NOW"

Max Sr. grabs his son right arm and slips him in the face by yelling at him in disrespectful.

"Who the hell you think you are yelling at him that way I'm sorry I had a bad day to your mother almost knock my head by throwing a chair at me."

"Why what happened in there?"

"Let's just say she is going to take you away from me & I wasn't going to let that happened."

Max Jr. sat down on the couch getting more bad news that is destroying his family what his dad was telling him. He begins to start crying on why all these horrible thing are happening to him & his father.

Looks like your actions in court & me getting black ball at Darcy's funeral was the same said Max Jr.

"How so?" said his father.

"We both lost our women" said Max Jr.

Max Sr. sat down with his son showing his feeling and remorse to his son letting him know that he's not long in his days of darkness. But very soon both Colars will turn their grieves into rage against the world that dumps them.

We Drift

The next day with all the grief & gloomy still clouded the life both colars a knock was on the front it was a sheriff and movers was there. Max Jr. woke up walk down stair rubbing his eyes & yawing he opens the to see the sheriff and moving truck.

Is there something wrong sheriff? Said Max Jr.

Yes is your father here? Said the sheriff.

Yes he's still sleeping? Said Max Jr.

Can you go wake him up for me? The sheriff

Sure. Said Max Jr.

Max Jr. walks back upstairs to get his father to come on down stairs for another horrible that awakes them both. He knock on his bedroom to begin calling him.

Dad?

What do you want?

Theirs a sheriff asking for you?

He opens his bedroom door runs down stairs with his boxer brief and white tank top rush to the door to see what's going on.

Sheriff what's going on here?

I'm here because you haven't paid your house note so you and your son are being evicted. Said the sheriff.

Wait what there's must be some kind of mistake they say I would have a couple of days to make my payment. Said Max Sr.

Look I just lost my job, my wife, & just about to lose my son please I'm begging you not to put me & my son out . Said Max Sr. so despaired to the sheriff.

Sir I'm sorry that you & your son are having a tough time but I have to do my job by making you and your son to be evicted go head movers.

The movers came inside and begin moving all the furniture's start from the living room to upstairs while both Max's watch with sadness & disappointment. They force to be put out while the mover's continues there business.

Dad what's going here, why are we putting out in the streets? Said Max Jr.

We got evicted they wouldn't give another chance to make payments.

So where are we going?

Nowhere let's keep walking. Said Max Sr.

As both colars kept on walking on the sidewalks in the freeway they was homeless, hungry & desperate for a place to stay for that day. As frustrated that Max's dad was going threw he was determent to get a ride so he & his son could get out the heat. Both father & son use their thumbs for hitchhiking 12 minutes later a car pulls up it was a senior couple who save them by giving them a ride.

Thank you so much Max come on. Said his dad .

You're both welcome where are you two headed? The old man ask.

Ugh were actually looking for a place to stay for the night because we have just been evicted today.

Oh my god that's awful? Said the old woman.

Awl man I'm so sorry Mr.-

Colar , Max colar this is my son Max Jr.

Hi Max Jr. said the old woman

Hi. Said Max with sadness in his voice.

Everything is going to be alright because you and your father can spend a night at our house. Said the old man.

How old are you son?

He's 17 years old ma am. Said Max Sr.

Our oldest granddaughter is 17 years old too said the old lady.

The old lady went inside her purse pulls out her wallet to show Max Jr. show her lovely blonde hair eyes granddaughter to brighten up Max Jr. He crack a smile until his father quickly snatch the picture away from his son to take a look at the young lady.

What's her name? Said Max Sr.

Her name is Carmen, said the old lady.

Carmen said Max Sr. as he breathe heavily with calm.

Everybody pulls up to a one story brick house every Max Sr. & Jr. got with seems to be grateful. Both men bath in different bathrooms the old lady prepared these drifters and her husband a wonderful meals. Such as baked chicken, mashed potatoes with brown gravy, broccoli, & with dinner rolls all four plates sat at the table. The old lady grab the colars clothes to put them in the washer machine to be wash with other clothes. They got out the separated bathrooms Max Sr. was wearing the old man robe and Max Jr. was wearing the old lady purple robe. His father looks at him and begins to laughs at him as he walk in the hallways.

They walk toward the kitchen and sat down at the table to bless the food in silence. Everybody begins passing the food around to fixing their plates. The colars enjoy the homemade cooking that they have not had in a long time. After finishing the delicious homemade feast the old lady got their clothes out the dryer and ironing their clothes with a scent of snuggles. They sat down in the living room watching a football game on the cotch. Once the game was over everybody in the house went to bed colars share a bed together in the guess room. 30 minutes later Max colar Sr. got up to wake his son up to leave the old couple's house. They grab their clothes of the iron to put them on and their shoes too in the mind of survivor of Max Sr. He force his son to go inside the bedroom of the good hearted elderly couple to steal their wallets and pocket books. In the dark hallway Max Sr. grab the two items to snatch all the money out. Max Sr. also sneak inside the bedroom going over to the old man night stand open the dresser to get unexpectedly handgun of 44 magnum desert eagle pistol.

It gave Max Sr. a boost like "who's going to fuck with me" attitude then Max Jr. went inside their closet to get some of their duffle bags.

They slide out the backroom window like thieves and sparing their lives they took a taxi to go to a nearest bus station. They got on where the bus driver announced everybody is headed to Arizona where they will turn pain and agony turns into an unexpected rage of blood bath.

Welcome to Arizona Colars

After a 10 hrs. & 45 minutes of bus riding everybody including the colars got off to step into a new state hoping for new & improve life in the Grand Canyon state. The Colars walk into a store to buy coffee and have a chat with one another.

So Max how do you like Arizona so far? Said Max Sr.

We just go here dad, so I don't know? Said Max Jr.

How much money did get from those people? Said Max Jr.

We about 200$ left? Max Sr.

200$ by the end of today that money is going to be all gone? Said Max Jr. as he lean toward to his father.

Don't worry about that I going to have everything all worked out? Said Max Sr.

"What about a job or me am I going back to school"?

Max the things I'm about to teach you want need public schools no more.

What do you mean by that dad?

You'll see! Said his father.

As they remain in their seat to drink their coffee Max Jr. has no idea what kind of man that his father is going to be and put him through. Four minutes later they got finish their coffee walk out the store to begin a long walk in 99 degrees heat with a little money and little hope.

They kept on walking until they stop to rest their feet. Max Jr. went inside the stolen duffle bag to pull out a large bottle of warm water to begin drinking. His father grab the water bottle away from his son he decide to drink it with a little of dehydrate he was suffering. They both stop resting and begin walking until a man in a SUV stop to ask them for a ride.

You guy need a ride? Said the guy

Yes we do, can you please help us? Said Max Sr. with a fake concern in his voice.

Please, please come on in both of you? Said the man with kindness in his heart.

Thank you so much? Said Max Jr.

They got inside the car to get out the burning heat of the day.

So where you guys headed Mr.-?

Colar, Max this is my son Max Jr. where ever you can take us.

My name is Stevenson Phil.

Is Phil is your last name? Said Max Jr.

Phil laughs at Max Jr. for his humor and he answer back at him to continue his questions with the two drifters.

That's good young man real good I needed that laugh said Phil.

"Where headed to the city to find a place to stay for the day". Said Max Sr.

I'm headed to Coconino that's where I stay said Phil.

As Phil continues driving they show up to this hotel called "Days Inn" they got out go inside to get a room. After they got a room for the night the colars began to unpacking with stolen clothes Max Jr. goes inside one duffle bag to pulls out a the stolen desert eagle with 8 rounds while Max's dad is in the bathroom. When the bathroom begins to open Max Jr. quickly put the huge gun back inside the bag to start watching television.

What were you doing Max?

Nothing I was just moving the bags around to I can see t.v.? Said Max Jr.

Why we can't have a phone or a cellphones? Said Max Jr.

We don't need no phones because all we is each other son? Said Max Sr.

That night while Max Jr. was asleep in his hotel bedroom his dad got up went to a lobby to get a drink of beer. Until he see a fancy suit businessman wearing a ballon bleu de cartier watch that caught the eyes of Max Sr. He kept his eyes on the unknown businessman for whole night after he finish his vodka. When he got up from his chair Max Sr. turn his head to hide his face. Once he walk out the hotel Max Sr. follow him to the very back parking lot. Max Sr. runs up pulls out his desert eagle to hit him at the back of the head to knock him out cold.

He ran through the guy's pockets to pull his smartphone to slam him on the ground feeling like he's going to get up. He takes off the guy's cartier watch to put it on his wrist and he pulls a wallet to steal 1000 dollars. He ran to dark bushes to hide out when a local police show's up but not looking for any trouble. Max Sr. was on his way to become one of the most ruthless criminal in Arizona and his son will follow.

Later that night Max Sr. went back to hotel with stolen watch and cash in hand while his son still asleep he put everything inside the bag to go to sleep in his hotel bedroom.

Good Times With Father & Son

The next morning Max Jr.'s dad woke him with excitement in his voice telling & showing his son the money he found & a special gift to his only beloved son.

Look what I got Max? Said Max Sr.

What? Said Max as he got up from his bedroom.

I found 1,000 dollars and a watch? Said his father.

Where dad?

Never mind where I found it, it's ours now. Said Max Sr.

Look here grab some of these covers & pillows to put them inside the bags except for this one. Said Max Sr.

Why? What's so wrong with this one? Said Max Jr.

No reason just don't touch this bag no matter what you here. Said Max Sr. to his son.

Unware that Max Jr. knows what's inside the duffle that his father never show him. The Colar's pack everything paid for the room until they seen a police. But Max Sr. remain clam as he made the payment the ambulance came to pick up the man in the suit on the stretcher still he remain unconscious with blood on the back of his head. Max Sr. calls for a cab to pick them up from the Days Inn twenty five minutes later a cab came to get them. No officers look or even questions the two guys that left in the taxi.

Where you guys headed? Said the taxi driver.

Take us to a bus station? Said Max Sr. with a smile on his face.

The taxi driver takes them to the bus station and drop them out off they got back on a bus to go to phoenix. After a couple of hours of bus riding the got off to take another taxi cab to go to E Main St, Mesa, AZ. They show showed up with bags and cash to rent a car 2008 white Dodge Charger they paid in cash for two weeks. They ride out to do some sight-seeing for the first time in a long time both father & son were having a time of their lives listing to One Republic "Counting Stars". Max Jr. opens a glove department and found an old school digital Kodak camera and seen only have three films left.

Max Sr. asked his son "What's with the camera"?

Oh, this old thing it only have three films left?

Let's take the picture? Said his father.

Max Sr. pulls the car over to the side road his son rewind the camera with excitement blooms in the air they both smile to do selfies to stamps the one of the greatest memory in their lives. His father pulls the car back on the road to begin their traveling.

They travel to the Grand Canyon out of there to set on their car hood basket in the beautiful sight-seeing of blue skies, white & gray clouded skies. They would take turns on taking pictures on one of the most must see views in their lives. His son asked him can he take a picture of him and the Grand Canyon he agree. Max Sr. took the camera to take the picture of his only friend & beloved son with a smile on his face.

After Max Sr. took his son's picture they went to their next visit hoover dam to see more excitement in their only happy times. Couple of miles later they got out to move into a little crowd of tourist but Max Jr. wanted to take a picture of father alone with the hoover dam.

"Move over to the right dad ".

What over here ok? Said his father

Yeah stay right there & smile. Said his Max Jr.

Great. Said his Max Jr.

Ok kid we let's go and get something to eat?

Where?

Let's find a place around here ok?

They got back inside their car play the radio on a pop station to enjoy their perfect day. They found a place called Mile High Grill at Main Street Jerome. They took a set at a table ordering their meal Jr. order the diablo burger with a mug root beer. His father order the ribeye steak with an alcohol called "The Snow". After having finishing their dinner they remain sitting at their table watching the sun goes down as the skies follow.

I love this dad I wanted here forever?

I know & we will son.

When the night came they finally got up to get back inside their car to begin driving for a place to stay for a couple of days. They arrived at a hotel called "Oak Tree Inn" to get settle in once they got a room they ended their wonderful day with beers Max Jr. was happy that he got a little freedom from his father. But Max Jr. have no idea that he and his father are going to create an unexpected nightmare in the Grand Canyon state.

From Robbery to Murder

The next morning as the sun awaken both guys from their sleep they got up stretching and yawing. Max Sr. got to wash his face & use the bathroom while Max Jr. is walking to the restaurant to get something to eat. 10 minutes later his father came to the restaurant to join his son for breakfast and to talk about what to do for the day.

Dad, what are going to today?

I don't know?

So how much money do we have left?

Not enough?

Are you going to find a job?

His father laughs quietly at his son's question.

Just finish up your breakfast ok we got a long & fun day ahead of us.

Like what dad?

I don't know but today is going to much different?

How different?

You'll see Max, you'll.

As Max Jr. finish up his breakfast they paid for their meal they got inside their rental car and drove into town to do a little bit of shopping. Max Jr. went to Macy's to buy some jeans & few t-shirt then he found a black hoodie to suit his looks & personality. Meanwhile his father went to a hunting store to get some hunting clothes and boots all black. After

Max Sr. some night time hunting clothes he went to a pawn shop to pawn the cartier watch and get 4000 dollars for it. Then he decide to buy two guns one a KP-02 Sig Sauer P229 and an Uzi.

Max Jr. meet up with his father at a parking lot and went a shocked look on his face he sees two deadly guns that he has no idea what his father had in mind. He ask his father questions when they got inside their cars.

What these guns for are we to war?

Let's just say we have to protect ourselves?

Who's coming after us?

No one we just have to protect ourselves?

I-I-I- see. Said Max Jr. with stuttering in voice because he was getting scared for what to come.

Later on that cool clear night sky the Colars prepared themselves for a night that will change their lives for the worst. Both of them take turns taking shower dress in all black pants, boots, long sleeves sports shirt & black gloves to match the night. Max Sr. his son grab the bags full of clothes and guns to put inside the trunk of the car. They travel to a local suburb to begin they're unexpected reign of terror on a peaceful neighborhood. Max Sr. Park the car down the street pop the trunk to get two pistols and sneak inside house number 1 to slip inside the back window to while a neighbor's dog is barking.

Max Jr. follows his dad upstairs to inside a master bedroom of two couple who are dead asleep. As Max Jr. keeps an eye open of the door his begins to steal more money from out of the dresser. They both exist from the bedroom and walk down stairs to the kitchen and grab some beer & some lobster tails. After eating the home owner food and drinking their beer with both smiles on their faces they went back out the back window & left the neighborhood.

On that same night they went inside the another neighborhood where they continue burglaries they park their car two blocks down from the house that are going to break in. but this time Max Jr. was going to break in the house first time by jumping over the fence and opening the back door. They pull out their guns and slowly creep up the stairs until a little girl turns on the hall lights on to go the bathroom.

Both men froze at the bottom stairs like they have been identified two minutes later the little girl came out the bathroom rubbing her eyes went back to bed but did not the two men at the stairs.

Max Jr. took a deep breathe to being enter inside the master bedroom to find some money or jewelry as his father guarded the doorway with desert eagle making sure that no one will stop them even a little girl. With a little bit time sinking down his father silently hurry him up. Max Jr. went over to woman side of the bed slide his hand threw the bed mattress and pulls out some money. They quickly and quietly rush back down stairs until they seen a police car flashing with sirens thinking that someone might have spot them. They ran back out the back door run back to their car to drive off thinking that the cops were after them but they wasn't.

The night was not over yet they have one more house to invade to as the colars pulls the one house that was surrounded by the desert. Max Sr. told his son to stay inside the car so no one want steal it Max Jr. agrees. As his father sneak around the house a dog was back there he pulls out his desert eagle and shoot the dog three times. Max Jr. got out the car but did not say or scream a word.

Then Max Jr. heard a loud shout of "where's the money" then two shoots went inside the house. Max Jr. froze in horror as he sees the homeowner crawling in his front yard begging for help Max Jr. was still shock in disbelief. Max's father ran out the front door and put three more rounds into the helpless victim.

Max Sr. drag his son back into their car to drive of the property Max Jr. have now witness what was the guns for what he though was going to be the end but have no idea that it was the beginning of his father murdering rampage across the city.

We Can't Go Home

After Max Sr. made his first killed, he drove his son into the desert while Max Jr. begins to cry on why did his father had to kill. Max Sr. pulls the car over to have a word his only beloved son about what they have to do to survive.

"Why are you crying "?

"Why did you killed that guy "?

"I not going to let no one tell on us so I had to kill him"?

"So we are going to kill everyone who comes in our way"?

"Only if people know what we know?"

"Dad I-I-I want to go home let me stay with mom"?

Max Sr. pulls the car over to have a word with his son on his society and his thoughts on the world that they lived in.

"Max let me tell you something as a matter of fact get out the car?"

"Why you going to kill"?

"Only if you don't get out to listen to me?"

Max Jr. got the car and they began to talk with stars shining and the moon was full with darkness holds the night.

"Max here something you should, when me and your mom move to California we thought that everything was going to be great and it was. Things really go amazing when you came into this world but as we all grew as a family thing went from perfect to worst when she cheated on me with that guy. The life in California have close their doors on us and took our love away from us. That society would and will not give us another chance but in our society we are taking no chances, no waits, and most of all no remorse. Beside your mother didn't want you if she did that means she just want to send you to orphan.

So I'm stuck with you for the rest of my life?

Yes, I'm your father I will always be with you because I love you. Said his father.

What happens if I tried to get away for you? said

You want because I will die without you, you want left me died Max, wouldn't you?

Max Jr. shakes his head in a no way.

So we are starting our retribution on any one who will dare's to stop us?

It has already began son.

After Max Sr. gave his a survival and desperation speech he gave his son a hug for three minutes then they both got inside the car. He turns on the radio to hear ACDC "night prowler" to end their horrible and scary night boosting his father's ego. As they both drives back on the desert Max Jr. now knows that he can't get away if he does it will him own life. They also stop at a local restaurant to get some to eat as if nothing happened.

They next day on a beautiful sunny hot morning a local paperboy did some deliveries on his mop head. Everything went good for him until he saw a dead body lying in the front yard with bullet holes in the back of his back. After he breaks from his shock he goes inside his pocket pulls out his smartphone to call 911. Once he makes the call he stayed there with the body as he was instructed by the operator waiting on the police and ambulance. This kid has no idea that a father and son are going on a robbery and killing spree on any one that gets in their way.

About twenty minutes later a clan of officers shows up at the crime where the paper boy stood there he begins to explain on how he found the body with Det. Richardson.

"Now tell again what time did you make the call?" Said Det. Richardson

At 11: 00?

11: 00 ok do you happened to see anyone else who call for help?

No, detective just me?

Ok did you by all means take anything from the house before you made the call?

No sir?

Ok that all the question I have for you, so you free to go

After detective finishing up his questions his partner and him walk inside the house of the slain owner they see bloody hand prints on the wall on of the stair way as he tried to escape. They walk up stair to the bedroom to see everything clean and neat look outside the back window to see a slain dog in the back yard. Both officers have seen the aftermath of the murders but have no idea that a father & son from out of town has done this.

Max Jr. Gets His Cherry Squash

On that same afternoon at a different hotel in front of the desert mountain Max Jr. and his derange father sat in their rooms looking at t.v. together. Until his father got up to pulls out uzi to check the bullets in the chambers as Max Jr. look over with fear & worried in his eyes he begins to his father on what to do next.

What's with the uzi for dad?

I told you that we are taking no chances.

So we can't take any chances by getting something to eat?

Max Sr. puts a slight smirk on his as he continues to clean his gun.

Sure, it see why not.

Do you need anything while I'm out?

Just get some Jack Daniels on your way out?

I-I-I can't get that I'm only 17 years old.

I don't give a damn if you the same age as the pharaoh get me the fucking Daniels?

Wha? Said Max Jr. with trembling fear in his voice.

Max Sr. got up from the bed walk over to his son with the uzi in his hand then he puts his spare hand on his son's shoulder he laughs at him.

I'm just kidding, just kidding Max lose it up a little ok no I don't want anything just don't – be careful ok. Said Max Sr. with a smile heinous smile on his face.

As Max Jr. walks out the hotel room he got inside the white dodge charger to get something to eat at a local fast food restaurant. Couple of minutes he pulls up and gone inside to order his meal as he order his hamburger with French fries. Once he order his food his eye's froze into shock when he saw a 5'4 beautiful ginger hair young woman with turquoise eyes named "Amanda Neff" wearing a Kimchi Blue Satin Cross-back Cami top, Taryn Denim cutoff short bottom, wearing Aurora braided T-strap sandal with Ecote- scout panama hat. Stunning everyone inside including young drifter Max Jr. when he got his meal he sat down and began to eat.

While he continues to eat he continues to look at the beautiful Amanda as she eats with her friends. She looks up at Max Jr. as he quickly puts his head down with shyness she began to smile with her friends. Max Jr. once again began back looking at her but this she wave her hand and fingers at him he also wave his hand back at her then she calls him over for conversation.

Hi sweetie?

Hi?

What's your name?

Max, and you are?

I'm Amanda Richardson, but these friends of mine.

Her nickname is Manda. I'm Laura, I'm Kelly, and I'm Tracey.

Hi nice to meet you all.

So do you live around here Max?

Huh no I'm from out of town.

Really from where?

California.

Where you all from?

Here in Arizona.

You are so beautiful do you model or something?

As a matter of fact I do some acting and singing well, we all do.

Did you all go to some talent school?

Yeah, how did you know wait let me guess you knew?

Now, let me ask you something what do for a living?

I'm a survival.

Are you using a destiny child song or something?

As everyone laughs including Max.

Do you have any plans for tonight Max? Said Amanda.

No, why?

I just want to know that do you want to hang out or something?

Sure, yeah please with excitement his voice with the girls laughing.

After they finish up their meals they all got up but Max took their trey to empty to be a gentlemen and Amanda gave Max her number to call they gave each other hugs and said I see you later. As the night came Max call Amanda to meet up at the hotel where Max was staying at. She came over alone walk to his room to pay him a visit she knocks he opens the door to let her in. But this time she dress sexier for him by wearing a Rachel Roy sleeveless jumpsuit with high heels.

Wow you look great Manda?

Thanks Max are you here alone?

Huh, yeah I'm.

Ok.

Ok so what do you want to do?

She pulls out a joint from her purse to show her idea.

You want to smoke this with me?

Of course you do that?

Yeah I may be pretty but I'm not square?

She pulls out the lighter to smoke it she takes to puff then pass it to Max he also takes a puff as they both of their eyes begins to daze at each other and laughs.

You are the coolest girl I ever met?

Thank you're double C's?

What's that?

Cool & Cute silly.

Max laughs and begin to blush.

So Max do you have a girlfriend?

No, I mean yes I mean kinda?

What happened to huh?

Darcy, she was killed in a car crash when she was talking to me.

I'm so sorry was you and her was real close?

Yeah in a way of all the in my school she was the only one that was real nice to me. Said Max.

What grade are you in?

I'm a Junior how did you know I was school?

You can't lie I know who's in school

What grade are you in Manda?

I'm 20 years old.

I never hang out with a 20 year old?

Never, are you a virgin?

Why would ask me that?

Because you look so unexperienced?

That's not funny. They both begin to laughs with weed buzz in their system.

But all jokes aside I'm really am a virgin.

Amanda begin to hold his hand as intimacy started to grow in their high but that moment was crushed when his father came in to interrupt their moment when he closes the door.

Whoa who's this son?

I though you said you didn't stay with your father?

I'm sorry, I just wanting to have you all to myself Manda?

Hey, hey, hey, don't let me interrupt this lovely moment I'll tell you both what why don't I stay here while the two of you have you all personal time to yourselves?

Great, Mr.-?

Colar, Max Colar.

Did you name your son after you?

Yes I did, and you are lovely?

Amanda Richardson?

Right, but first let me get some things out of the car then I'll let you two go?

When Max's father walk out the room he went outside to get his some things from the car. Both Max Jr. & Amanda finish up their joint to walk out the room with highness but Amanda have made a mistake by leaving her purse in the hotel room. As they left went inside the car to drive out the desert so they can pick up where they left off. Max Jr.

& Amanda got out the car to set on top of the hood where she leans her head on his right shoulder to talk some more.

This night is so beautiful Max your dad seems pretty cool.

Oh you have no idea?

No idea of what ?

No comment.

What he's not dangerous is he?

He's just scary?

Oh please my father is scary?

How?

He's so fucking authority?

Like what, he's in some type of service?

Look, Max let's stop talking and let really do what we came here to do?

Like what kissing?

No silly, I mean fucking you?

What?

We can do it in & out the car but as long you go in & out of me?

Let's go inside the car it's getting chilly out here?

Ok.

Once they both got back inside the car Amanda begins to kissing his ear putting his hand between her legs. She says one more thing before they get started.

I'm starting to get wet?

His father pops out from the back seat grabbing her hair scaring her and his son loving the idea that she have's for Max Jr.

"WHAT ARE YOU DOING, LET HER GO NOW DAD"?

As he continues coking her he pulls her from the back seat trying to force himself on the girl. As she continues to fight for her life she bit between his legs to free herself from the car. He yells at his son to get her, she yells out for help but no one is there to help her in the dark, cold night. Amanda get knock upside the head by Max Sr. with his pistol. He drags her unconscious body back to the car he walk over to the car pulls his son out of the car as he froze in fear on what his father have done.

Max Sr. told his son to watch and learn on what he is going to do. He rips her clothes to get himself hard to begin to rape her first after he cum inside of her. With his pants still hanging off of him he grabs his son's shoulder to bring him over to Amanda's body.

Now it's your turn to go in & out of her?

No, I want do it ?

Look if you don't it then I'll go for seconds and I'll kill you?

As his father place the gun on top of his head so he begins to unzip his pants went down on top of her to begin having sex with her unconscious body just as he screams at his son by saying "HARDER, HARDER, and HARDER". She begins to awake screaming at him his father walk over to shoot her in head with her blood splashing on his face. He drags his son back inside the car to drive off this was the night that Max Jr. first time was the worst time of his life.

My Daughter Is Missing

On the next morning Amanda's mom calls her cell phone but with no answer so she tries again to make the call but still no answer. She turns to her husband who Det. Richardson is waking him up to discuss on no answer.

Charles, Charles, Amanda is not picking up her phone?

Ok, she might be sleeping so let her sleep and you do to.

I can't because I feel there's something wrong she always call.

Stop worrying & go back to sleep. Said Charles Richardson

She did just that and few minutes later she got up went downstairs to make her husband and her missing daughter some breakfast. He also got up reached over to the nightstand grab his cellphone to start calling her daughter it rings and rings but no answer even though there was no answer he also starting to feel their something wrong but he ignores it to get dress for work and walk downstairs to eat breakfast. As he sat down to eat Mary, Amanda's mother who continues to call her but still no answer she was getting frustrated in the kitchen.

No call, Mary?

No, this is so strange?

It is I just called her and there was no answer either?

Something is not right Charles she never done this before?

Det. Charles Richardson got from the table walk over to Mary put his arms around her to comfort her.

Hey, hey, calm down she's a grown woman if she's ever in trouble she'll gives us a call remember that time her car battery died along with her cell phone we both though that she was kidnapped and we put posters of her picture in the stores & on people cars. The next day she came back with the missing picture of her and ask for the reward.

They both begin to laugh at their past on what she's done.

So that's all it is she come to pop up at the house ok

Ok

I'm the meanwhile just wait by the phone when she calls you me ASAP.

He kiss Mary as he heads out the front door to report to the police station when he got there his partner Det. Thomas Wyatt starts talking about the shooting victim from yesterday morning. Det. Richardson sat down to take a deep breathe.

What's wrong Richardson?

Amanda didn't call us this morning?

Her car went dead again?

I don't know, but she'll come by the house just like last time so what do we have?

Oh, come to find out those bullets came from a desert eagle?

Desert eagle? Wow.

Yeah I just found out there was two homes that where burglarize?

By the same guy who killed that gentleman and his dog?

We don't know nobody who seen the intruder so?

So? What?

We don't have any connection from burglarize to murder.

Look you can figure all this out meanwhile let me call my wife to see did she call her back.

As he did just that while his partner steps out to get some coffee for himself and his partner as he calls his wife. Back at the hotel were both Colars stayed at a local house keeper named Lucinda Vargas she knocks on the door to say "Servicio de limpieza but no one answers. So she opens the door so see the filth and begins to go to work she started in the bathroom scrubbing the toilet, sink, and the bathroom then she move to the main room begin to changing the sheets, picking up all trash from the ground. She continues to picking up from the ground until she sees a cartier watch to put it inside the bag.

She begins to see a wallet she opens it up to see a young redhead young woman named "Amanda Richardson" in she also put that inside the bag as well and remain cleaning until she made her way inside the closet to see a large bag. She opens them to see two guns inside an Uzi and P229 she got out the room to call her manger so she can show him what she seen they both got out went to the front to call the police. Two hours later Det. Richardson and Det. Wyatt the cops came back to the hotel to find out what is the problem the manger explain.

My housekeeper name Lucinda Vargas called me inside the room to tell me look at this? Said the hotel manager.

I said "Oh my god"?

Who lived in this room?

The hotel manager ran back to the front room and pull up the record to see a guess name "Steven Starr". One of the officers went inside the bag to pull out the purse to see who is it, he was so shock that he ran to Det. Richardson to him what he had found.

Excuse detective there something you might need to take a look?

What?

He opens up the wallet to his daughter wallet he was furious he walk back inside the room to demanding to find his missing daughter went inside the bag to see the guns but the desert eagle. He ask the hotel manager what does this Steven Starr look like and do not play any games he said it's a white guy with a kid. Then Det. Richardson walk back to the hotel securing room to see the security as he saw the video he saw a man with a teenager in his mind he believe that he has found the prime suspect to his missing daughter case.

The Colars Meet the Willison

On that same day on being back on the road again Max Jr. has been quiet since his father killed the only girl free from sexual existing. His father turns on the radio to end the silence in their ride but Max Jr. quickly turns the radio off. His father once again turns back on the radio so he can hear some music as Max Jr. tries to reach for the nob his father grabs desert eagle to cock it of warning that if he tries to turns it off he might possible shoot his hand. Max Jr. looks at his father knowing his freedom has been out the window since the rape of Amanda of last night. As they kept on driving smoke rise from the hood of the car Max Sr. pulls the car over pop the hood to see what the problem is.

He waves his hand over to the engine to clear the smoke from the car as his son stays inside the car not coming out the car to see what it is until he walk over to the passenger side with the still inside his pants pocket. He pulls it out and knock on the window to call him out to help him on their car problem. He get out and follow his dad around the front.

What happened now dad?

I don't I'm trying to what the problem is but it's still smoking so when it clears were both going to fix the problem?

Ok, can I get back inside the car?

No you are going to do as I say?

As Max Jr. stays with his father in the burning heat in the desert minutes later the smoke clears Max Sr. opens the radiator cap and come to find out there was no antifreeze inside. He tells his son to go the trunk and find some antifreeze he did as he open the trunk but there was no antifreeze inside. Then an out of nowhere a van with family of four shows up to a young man.

You need some help, son?

Yeah, huh my car just ran hot could take me and father to town?

Where is your father, sweetie?

I'm here I was just checking on the side tires because it has a slow leak?

Do you need a ride Mr.-?

Colar, Max Colar and my number 2 junior.

Nice to meet you Max Colar and number 2?

And yes we do need a ride.

Please come in?

They both go inside the van with the family but they have no idea that the one of the drifters was going to make to nice family of travelers to be a living hell.

Thank you so much-?

Willison Paul, Willison this is my lovely wife Mandy Willison.

Hi again.

Who are these two little ones here?

That's Michael and Beth.

Hi Michael and Beth Max say hi to the kids?

HI, kids?

So where you people heading?

I was about ask you that were heading to local hotel because we're going to the Grand Canyon.

Have two been there?

Yes ma'am, we been there couple of days ago?

It so beautiful especially when the sun set.

Oh I bet it is?

While the dangerous Max Sr. plays nice to his victims the kids begins to argue about different movies that want to see separately. They voice started to get higher and higher in their arguing Max Jr. begins to shout at them. The van stops everybody stairs at Max Jr. when the kids begins to cry Mandy Willison talks to Max Jr. about shouting at the kids.

HEY, don't you ever yell at by babies who do you think you are?

Max Sr. pulls out the desert eagle to defend his son and hold the family hostage they trip went from good to bad. When Paul tries to talk to Max Sr. with ease to protect his family.

Who the hell you think you are yelling at my son bitch?

Mr. please don't shoot us we will not call or go to the police about this matter?

I know you want so just keep driving to the hotel and there want be a problem ok?

The Willison's continues driving as hostages of Max Sr. little Michael & Beth started to cry again. Max Jr. starts rubbing the kids arms saying to them softly that everything is going to be alright. Couple of miles later the Willison show's up to their hotel.

Everybody keep calm and get out the car quietly! Said Max Sr.

They all got quietly as Max Sr. demanded Paul walks toward the front office with Max Sr. standing right beside him watching every move he make. While Max Jr. holding Mandy's hand with the kids projecting the image of a happy family. Once Paul got the hotel key Max Sr. told him and his family to keep walking towards the room. They got there and not knowing that the family will not get out the room alive.

Alright Mr.Colar we did what you said just let us go please?

Yes, you did but unfortunately I change my mind.

What do you mean? Said Mandy with tears in her eyes holding her kids.

My lovely people we can't let you all leave. Said Max Sr.

PLEASE, PLEASE, PLEASE just let us were begging you? Said Paul on his knees.

Dad jus-?

Shut up Max I'm trying to teach you that we take no more chances in life?

Everybody begins to cry until they heard a knock on the door Max Sr. rushing to the door pushing everyone away including the crying kids. It was the housekeeper Max Sr. snatched the towels from her then closes the door.

Now where was we?

Dad let these people go they didn't do anything to us let them go or else?

Else what Jr?

I will kick your ass?

Max Sr. begins to laughs at his son for finally standing up to him with hostages in the room.

I mean dad don't this, I don't need these people bloods on my hands ok.

You know what you're right you don't need these people blood on your hands I do it?

So he knocks out his son unconscious so he want see what he's going to do with the family. Max Sr. wake his son once he finishing up his massacre. As they run out the back door of the building they got inside the Willison van to drive off. Max Sr. left a very diabolical scene leaving the whole Willison family in a pool of blood including the children who was shot in the back the head each. The housekeeper came back to the room she knocks but no one answer. She use her master key to open she drops everything and screams at the top of her lungs when she's the slaughter family cover in blood. Max Sr. left have committed the most unholy murders in the state's history the Willison had no chance to face a heinous monster like a Max Colar Sr.

We Found a Body and Another

After the housekeeper witness the aftermath of a family murder she got on the phone to call 911. Few hours later the cops came including Det. Richardson and his partner Thomas Wyatt shows up at the scene questioning the house keeper on who might she have seen to done all this.

Ma'am did you know my any chance who might have done this? Said Det. Thomas Wyatt.

No sir? Said the house keeper.

Who about you sir? Said Det. House keeper.

No I was at lunch before she told me all this detective. Said the hotel manager.

Detective Richardson came in to move the officers away so he can get them to point out the suspects.

Hey on your security camera did it capture a man and a teenager with these people?

I'm not sure, but let us to go to check it out. Said the hotel manager.

As the hotel manager and both detectives walk towards the security room they started to rewind on the day that the Willison's check in with no surprise they both look at the recognizable guys from another hotel security camera.

It's them?

Who is them? Said the hotel manager.

These are the same guys that were are looking for? Said Det. Richardson.

You think they did it? Said the hotel manager.

That's what here to figure out? Said Det. Wyatt.

As they got the disc from the hotel security room they went back in the hotel room discussing that the same guys from the other hotel are connecting to this murder and their missing detective's daughter.

So these guys are just giving themselves away to us? Said Det. Wyatt.

Yes, these assholes are making marks on them but we don't know who they are or where they going and who they looking for? Said Det. Richardson.

Is Mary still calling you about you both daughter?

As detective Richardson was just about to on calling his wife about their daughter his cellphone rings it was his wife. Just when he was about to get good news she still let him know that Amanda is still missing and her cell phone went dead.

Did she called yet? Said Det. Richardson

No? Something is very wrong I'm getting scared find my baby? Said Mary with trembling in his voice.

I will, as soon I get to the station? Said Det. Richardson.

No luck, Charles? Said Det. Thomas Wyatt.

No, what we need to do is find these son of bitches to stop them.

Once they got done talking to each other they drove off with the video disc in their car. They got the face of the possible suspect who they believe is connected to all the murders. But they have no idea that the Colars was moving few steps ahead of them. Meanwhile in the desert a local beer drinking was walking in the area where Amanda was killed in. He stop to rest his feet as he continues drinking his beer he smelt a foul odor in air he follow the trial as he walked he seen a red hair girl lying dead with a hole in her forehead.

He begins to scream at the top his lungs running for help and vomiting that the odor sicken him. As he make his way to the local hotel where Amanda was last seen in. He told a local police about what he seen but the officer smelt beer in breathe. Instead of believing him he place him under arrest for public intoxication. When he put the beer drinking in the back seat he continues to tell the officer to go look at the dead girl in the desert. The officer agrees so besides taking him to the station he follow the where the body is. They got there and seen the dead redhead young lady the officer recognized her he got on the radio to call in. Two hours later the officer and ambulance show up with Det. Thomas Wyatt he walk to the ambulance door got inside to the victim. The missing victim was detective Richardson's daughter as he walk off he got on his cellphone to call his partner.

Yeah Wyatt?

Detective Wyatt took a deep breath as he begins his partner a shocking discovering of the missing girl.

We found her! Said detective Wyatt.

Detective Richardson got a ride from another officer just a half of hour he arrived on the crime scene. He stop the ambulance demand them to open the door once he open the door open the body bag he seen his only baby girl murder in cold blood shot in the head. He walk out took an officer knife stick beating the hell out an officer car.

He pain ran deep when he shatter the windows putting dents on the front car door and the back. When he stop he sat down in the desert with hurt and shame while his partner and others help him up as he continues crying inside the car.

Detective Wyatt drove his partner follows the ambulance to the hospital as they got Det. Wyatt open the door for his partner. He got still grieving over his daughter's death and sat down in the waiting room rubbing his eyes with a tissue.

Twenty minutes later his wife Mary shows up at the hospital with her brother and older sister got and continues to cry at her husband's arms. Mary fell down on the floor with her knees weaken her with her husband fell down with her.

As they found Amanda's body was decease the life of their daughter who brings joys, trust, and love that was gone forever. Threw the grieving Det. Richardson is determent to bring his daughter's killer and the Willison family murder to justice. In his mind the guys on the video known as the Colars that detective Richardson and Wyatt will soon meet face to face with one of them very soon.

Either You Kill Him Son or I Kill You

As Det. Richardson and his wife struggling for their daughter's death, the night came when the Colars continues to give death for those who dare to cross them. They continues driving in the stolen van that Max Sr. killed. He begins to talk to his son about now its turn to have blood on his hands because he feels that he done enough.

Max I'm sorry that I hit you unconscious but I couldn't give that family chance especially that bitch mother. Said Max Sr.

Don't apologize to me dad apologize to all your victims. Said Max Jr.

Aww come on Max we don't apologize if we do that means we are giving them chances, we don't give no chances so fuck all those motherfuckers. Said Max Sr.

Even those kids you killed they was so young they was innocent? Said Max Sr.

They were seeds of no chances that means they were part of the system that shout us out so it is what it is. Said Max Sr.

You're evil. Said Max Jr.

As they stop the conversation they continue to driving in the desert night until they got across the gas station the van had a flat tire on the driving side. Max Sr. look at his with a smile on his and told his son to find a spare tire in the back of the van. He did what he told as his father walk across the street to get some service and food and drinks. As Max Jr. went inside he look inside the van trying find a cell phone or any communication for help. Knowing and fearing that more people will die at the hands of his father the serial killer.

When Max Sr. got in line he had some beef jerky, skittles, big bag of nachos cheese chip, and two cans of monster energy. When he walk up to the counter placing his belongings in front of the cashier paying for his food. A man who look like a mechanic walk right behind Max Sr. he turns around to ask for road inset.

Hey are you a mechanic Sir?

Yes?

Good can you help me & my son out there across the street in that van? Said Max Sr.

Sure just let me buy these beers and I will be out there. Said the mechanic.

Do worry about it, I'll pay for it? Said Max Sr. with kindness in his voice.

While Max Jr. continues looking for a phone he heard his father talking to a mechanic he hurry up to find a tire but there was none available. He close the back door when his father came to the van with the help.

Dad I didn't any tires in here?

Don't worry about it we got help son?

You must be little Max? With his hand out for introducing.

Max shake this gentlemen hand?

He stick his hand out greeting the mechanic as his father told him so.

Pleasure. Said Max Jr.

So what's seems to be a problem Sir?

My front left tire gone flat?

The mechanic walk over to take a look he seen it and asking Max Sr. what do he want him to do and where they going. He got inside the tow truck gone round to back up the truck to the van to hook up the van with chains flat bed. Once the mechanic got done with his job all three men got inside the tow truck to drive off the night of the desert. The mechanic will soon fall at the hands of the Colars in this night.

So where you guys headed?

At a hotel? Said Max Sr.

Where?

Just a few miles ahead?

Ok, so where you guys from?

California.

Ok, so you guys are on vacation?

Vacation, yes.

As they continues talking Max Jr. seen a pistol in middle of the seat feeling like that he can end his father killing spree. His father looks at his son with a smile on his face as if everything will alright but it's not. When reach a couple of more miles out of nowhere Max Sr. pulls out his desert eagle to tell the mechanic to stop and get out of the truck at gun point. The mechanic got out and slowly grabs his gun to defend himself while Max Sr. drags him out the truck. The mechanic pulls his gun out to hit Max Sr. in face went back inside the truck demanded Max Jr. to get out.

With both Colars on their knees with arms behind their backs now they was hold hostage. Max Sr. finally got a taste of his own medicine. The mechanic heard some sires he turns his head and make a fatal mistake when Max Sr. scope up some sand and throws it at the mechanic's face to blind him and also knock him out. When the mechanic woke up his arms and legs where hog tie his face was facing a scorpion screaming for help.

The scorpion stings the mechanic in the nose injecting its venom inside. As Max Sr. laughs with a smoking a cigarette he turns his attention to the scorpion by walking over to squash it in front him. He still kept him hog tie calling his son to get out the truck and make his mark or should I say his first kill.

Max, Max by boy get over here?

What are you doing?

I'm not doing anything but you are.

What do you mean?

Now it's time you to become a man?

Be a man?

Yep here take his gun and kill him?

Max Jr. begins to shake his head because he knew that his father was going to force blood on his hands.

You don't have a choice he tried to kill me and you so you have to.

The mechanic begins to beg for his life screaming at Max Jr. don't do this, don't be like him. Max Sr. answer back at him by saying.

"YOU FUCKING IDIOT, HE IS LIKE ME HE'S A COLAR & US COLARS GIVES NO CHANCES".

He gives the gun to his son making him to shoot him, he looks at the mechanic in the eyes seeing the life of this man will come to the end my his hands. Max Jr. level the gun at him in the middle of his forehead getting ready to execute this man. He lower his gun down pulling himself together that he cannot committed this crime. A desert eagle was pointed at the side of his son head pulling the trigger to make the kill.

If you don't kill him then I will kill you this time?

He raise the gun back up while the mechanic starts to beg for his life again shouting "NO, NO NON- then a single shoot fired at his forehead with his brains splatter all over the cactus. Sick demisted Max Sr. yelling at the top of his lugs for his son first kill like he won the lottery.

THAT' BOY, YOU'RE FINALLY A MAN.

With shame and blood on his hand his father turns around to gives his son a kiss, Max Jr. quickly wipe it off as if he was infected. They got inside the tow truck riding off with their snacks and the mechanic's beer continue driving and killing anyone to satisfied the blood lust who is next on their murderous rampage.

The Colars Wanted Dead or Alive

The next morning of the day while the family & friends of Amanda Richardson said their goodbyes when they left the Valley of the Mortuary & Cemetery. As the Richardson got inside the limo Det. Charles Richardson got out the limo to walk over and talk to Laura, Kelly & Tracy on what happened on that day before Amanda was killed.

Mr. Richardson where sorry about Amanda? Said Laura as she's crying.

Sorry about what? Said Det. Richardson.

About that sh-. Said Kelly with tears in her eyes then she was cut off by the limo driver.

He turns his head looking at the limo driver as he walk towards with a message from his partner Det. Thomas Wyatt.

I'm very sorry sir of your interruption but there's a detective said he got something for you. Said the limo driver.

Ok I'm there. Said Det. Richardson.

What do you got Wyatt?

I just found that there was a camera inside a white dodge Charger and we have a clear shoot of these suspects. Said Det. Wyatt.

As he seen the suspects he begins to call Kelly and the girls over for some questioning about the guys inside the photo graphs.

Hey girls I got a picture here and I want to ask you all that was this the man or boy you probably seen Amanda with when you three? Said Det. Richardson.

As he shows the photograph of a young boy and his father inside the car Laura Kelly and Tracey went into total shock when they recognized one of the guys in the pictures.

THAT'S HIM, The kid on the right!

Are you sure? Said Det. Wyatt

Yes, that's him too he said his name Max I believe? Said Kelly.

Max what?

While getting into further information Mary got out the limo asking her husband what is going on here.

What is going here Charles? Said Mary

We got a name for one of the suspects of Amanda? Said Det. Richardson to his wife.

Who?

This kid name" Max"? Said Det. Richardson

Holy shit are you sure? Said Mary

Well the girls meet him when they gone to get food?

Ok, Wyatt go to the station and let everyone there knows these guys one of them name Max is the primary suspect along with his father. Said Det. As he got back inside the limo with wife Mary to go back home getting some rest from burying their daughter. At another hotel where the Colars was resting in Max Jr. turns on the TV a local news to a shocking news about a local red hair girl was found dead in the desert.

"This just a breaking news the police has released a picture of these men here who is connected to a murder was a detective's daughter name" Amanda Richardson" who was last scene. They are consider to be extremely dangerous and armed if you see these two please call your local police department I'm Catherine Hall with your evening news".

Max Sr. turns off the television looking at his like they have accomplished something in their lives to get everybody attention.

Congratulations son we hit the big time? Said Max Sr.

What no were wanted for murder and the most shocking part of all this that was a detective's daughter? Said Max Jr.

How do know that? Said Max Sr. while he cleaning his gun that he stole from the mechanic.

Because she said that he was an authority and she has his last name. Said Max Jr.

If what are saying is true then that means we don't go out in the daytime no matter what? Said Max Sr.

What about in the night time?

That's might be the only time we can to make our escape since were outlaws have to get out of Arizona tomorrow night at midnight. Said Max Sr.

In what?

We'll do what we always do Max steal a car and kill anyone who refuse to help us? Said Max Sr.

Remember do not go out during the day especially you because they know your name?

If you get to leave me your punishment will be more excruciating then all the other who came before us! Said Max Sr.

Putting fear into his son's eyes giving him his finale warning before they try to escape the state that they struck fear and terror to. They both finish there beers and go to bed while they got inside there separated bed Max Jr. begins to open his eyes looking at the stars in the night sky. He really felt trap that his own father who claim that he would never harm his only son will kill him if he shows his face to the public. Max Jr. was thinking how he can stop or get away from his malevolent father. But he will soon realize his ambitions to go for it even if it mean he will strike a deal with Arizona police department.

Max Jr. Gets Arrested

When the Max Jr. got up from his bed he sees his father woke up and gone to the bathroom to wash his face and peeing. He walk towards the front door quietly opens it and walks free towards the back door to escape his father's rage. As he continues walking to a local gas station watching for any cops that was looking for him & his father but he was cleared from any authority. Max Jr. goes inside the gas station the cashier knob his head on greeting Max Jr. he walk around to get some photos chip, energy can drink and asking the cashier for cigarette. Out of nowhere a cop shows up with his partner to get some gas for his car.

Max Jr. was caught and felt that there was no escape to go free and Max Jr. did not turn his head but he palms were sweating as he reached inside his pocket to pull out a ten dollar bill. The cashier begins to ask Max Jr. for his ID he goes back in his pockets but there was no driver license. He cancels the cigarettes but buys the food and drink he still didn't turns his head while the police was behind him. Max Jr. got his change and walk out as the cop kept looking at this mysterious young man. When he left the gas station he was felt so relief that the police officer didn't stop him to take a look.

Max Jr. clam was over when a police car begins to follow his a siren begins to go off to stop Max Jr. he stop walking but did not turn around then the police officer begins to talk to him.

Turn around? Said the officer

Max Jr. turns around slowly with fear in his spirit the cops got the car and begins to questioning him.

Is there a problem? Said Max Jr.

Yes it is, you're wanted for murder. Said the officer.

So turn right back around and put your hands behind your back as he read him his rights. Max Jr. begins to remember on what his father told him "do not go outside in the daytime." As Max Jr. get inside the car without putting up the fight that he couldn't win. Once they got to the station the local reporters turns their attention to one of the most notorious suspect in Arizona history.

"Were live with your afternoon new this just been a breaking news one of the suspect of multiple murders have been caught. A young man Max Colar Jr. but his father is still on the run and consider extremely dangerous." We have one down and one to go said the officer, the police are still researching for his father I'm Catherine Hall with your news.

After showing his face and name they took him inside the station to get put inside they system. Meanwhile back at the hotel room where his father was still there he got furious when he pick up the TV. And slam it on the floor for his son being so stupid and going against his father's will. When Max Jr. gone inside Det. Richardson walk up to Max Jr. and knock him the hell out before his men hold him back. Max Jr. got back up with his mouth all bloody up then he was place inside a holding cell about thirty minutes later an officer handcuff Max Jr. then escorted to an interrogation room for questioning.

As he sits there with an officer standing in the doorway Det. Richardson walk in to tell the officer wait outside. Det. Richardson pulls out a picture of his late daughter Amanda Richardson to show Max Jr.

"This girl was the most beautiful girl in this life and certainly in mines her life was perfect until you and your evil ass father put an end to her. Now give me one good reason on why I shouldn't kill you right now." Said Det. Richardson.

I 'am truly sorry about your daughter detective I never had no attention on murdering her. Said Max Jr.

Really, what was your attentions then? Said Det. Richardson

"Sex" Said Max Jr.

Detective Richardson yanks Max Jr. across the table like Batman did the Joker in dark knight.

"There is no cops here to stop me this time, I'll kill you right here & right now you little shit". Said Det. Richardson

You could, but it want bring Manda back? Said Max Jr.

Don't call her that only I can her that? Said Det. Richardson

What I did but showing my face to the public was stupid but I got myself arrest so your men can help me? Said Max Jr.

"What"! Said Det. Richardson

Yeah, that man in the picture my father is evil he's the devil he's the real killer you need?

What makes you any different than your father? Said Det. Richardson

I don't kill families, strangers, & rape girls? Max Jr.

Detective Richardson sat him down in his chair then Det. Wyatt walks inside the interrogation to join his partner in this investigation.

I just came back from the crime scene and all the bullets match from all the murders, so Maxy what kind of gun did your father use? Det. Wyatt.

I don't know he never told me or show me? Said Max Jr.

You know Mr. Colar we do have a death penalty here in Arizona, I'll tell you what you give us your father we'll reduce your sentence? Said Det. Wyatt

Just think about it Maxy I'm sorry Mr. Colar? Said Det. Wyatt

As they both detectives walk out to get some air they let young Max Jr. to sit there to think about his decision. This was Max Jr chance to put his own father away and to be free from him with this difficult decision he has to face in his dead end life.

Sorry Dad

That same night Max Jr. walked out the police station very mysteriously from the front door. With guilt & onus burying over his head Max Jr. continue walking at the hotel where he & his father were staying at. Once he got there the door was open he sticks his head threw the door quietly calling his father inside the dark room but no answer. Max Jr. walk inside the room tries to turn on the light but no lights came on including the bathroom he trip over busted TV that his father destroyed. But there was one more room that he didn't check it was the closet with sweat rolling down his face and his palms were sweating as well. He got closer & closer reach over to the door knob turns it around and opens it all he felt was nothing and saw darkness.

As Max Jr. continues to stand in front the closet he father slowly craws from under the bed like a snake not saying a word or making a sound as he creep from behind with a bed sheet. Then he threw it over his son's upper body with his son screaming then he viciously throws him against the walls and he turns him around to punch him the mouth. Max Sr. pick up his son's unconscious body carrying him in the dark ways of the hotel with blood on the floor into a dark basement. When Max Jr. got woke up he find himself tied up across the floor fearing for his life thinking that his father was going to kill him but he was going to get the worst kind of punishment that he never had.

Dad…what is this …? Said Max Jr. wiggling his arms.

His father lay down right next to him answering back at him.

You betrayed me? Said Max Sr. so quietly.

What.... No...I –I jus-? Said Max Jr. as he begins to cry.

"SHUT THE FUCK UP", you little shit I know? His father shouted at him.

Max Sr. got up walk on his crying son to go over a drawer of a desk top pulling out a leather bullwhip looking forward to his son some serious punishment for disobeying him. While his son raises his voice begging his father don't punishing him.

What did you tell the cops Max?

Nothing, I swear to God I didn't tell them nothing dad?

You're lying to me?

I promised dad, didn't say nothing?

Max Sr. squads down to rip his back shirt open to he got back up grabs his bullwhip and begins to whipping him over thirteen times until he bleed to death Max Jr. scream so loud that no one couldn't hear him accept him.

You look like Jesus at the Praetorium, son! Said Max Sr.

F-F-Fuck you, dad? Said Max Jr. barley talking.

No son fuck you for betraying me your father! Said Max Sr.

As he pulls out his gun and aim at him until he hears sirens and sees flashing lights. Then a voice at a megaphone appears it was Det. Richardson and Det. Wyatt and others

Mr. Colar your surrounded and got nowhere to go come out with your hands on top of your head and your son too. Said Det. Richardson

Max Sr. panic really hard that he walk up from the basement and look out the window to Arizona finest lined up with their guns pointed at the lowering hotel. He went back to the basement yelling for his son once he got back down there he escape and saw blood on the floor but didn't leave a trail of it.

"MAX OH MAX, COME OUTSIDE. DONT MAKE YOUR FATHER COME MORE ANGRY THAN YOU ALREADY HAVE!" Said, Max Sr looking for him.

You four take that side Det. Wyatt.

As the four officers make their way inside the hotel they use their flash lights to look for the suspects they search around to see nobody inside hiding they each yield "Clear " in every room. Two officers make their way towards the basement one officer open the door see Max Sr. he open fires at the two officers shot them dead at the doorway. Then two more officers follows the gun shots at the basement door. They got down there flashing there info red beam but only see shots fires at them Max Sr.

You, you, you, come with me? Said Det. Richardson.

No Richardson don't he want everyone to come inside there and shoot them all one by one. Said Det. Wyatt.

"Fuck that shit I'm not staying out here so my men getting killed that son a bitch killed my baby" Said Det. Ricardson.

Shit listen to me.

Detective Richardson and his men walks inside the hotel building yelling at Max Sr. demanding that he comes out to surrenders but there was no answer. They went down to the basement to see their fellow officers shot dead by the hands of Max Sr. Once they made their way Max Sr. pops out of nowhere to put the dead cop gun at the temple of Det. Richardson holding him hostage at will.

"Take all your clips out of your guns and throw them at me do it or this man will die". Said Max Sr.

Do it, Do it now damn it? Said Max Sr.

The officers did what they was told all of them took out their clips from out of their guns and another instruction was giving to them.

"Now empty all the bullets" said Max Sr.

They all empty out all the bullets from their magazines.

Now what, we did what you say let detective Richardson go?

Close the door? Said Max Sr

What?

Max Sr. ask one more question to the officers. "Where's my son "?

We don't know?

Detective please close the door so they want see this?

Detective Richardson close the door and Max Sr. also told him to lock it so they want escape. Max Sr. walk towards the front door with his hostage going face to face with Det. Richardson with a trade.

Look what I got?

What are you Mr. Colar?

Where's my son?

We don't know let him so we can find him?

No, you find my son so we can get out of here and may be we'll let him go tell your men to throw their guns at me, NOW said Max Sr.

Alright, we will throw them at him so there want be any bloodshed.

They all threw their guns at him and his hostage so they can make a deal.

I LIED! Said Max Sr.

Once he pulled the trigger Det. Richardson elbow him in the stomach and drags him on the ground as they wrestle so one of them to get the gun. Max Sr. head butts Det. Richardson out cold he picks up the gun pointed at him to say one more thing before killing him.

"You want me to tell you how quickly your dead bitch daughter came"?

I shot her in the head and I will do the same for you to once I tell you?

All of the officers begging him not to shoot him until a gun shot was fired in Max Sr. neck. He drops his gun holding his bleeding neck and starts chocking on his own blood and turns around to see the shooter it was his son Max Jr. he begins to cry to see his father shoot dead and falls on the ground. Max Jr. drops the gun continues crying saying quietly "I'm sorry dad, I love you". The officers and Det. Wyatt runs up to check on Det. Richardson and the remaining officers inside. Max Jr. was escorted to the cops car without handcuff but there was one more thing that he wanted to get off his chest it was the wire that Det. Wyatt put on him before he left the station that night. Max Colar Sr. murderous crime was over the state was relief that their perfect storm passed. Max Jr. got inside the car ride back to the station so he can be at peace and be safe on that night.

END